SPIRIT RANGERS

BY KARISSA VALENCIA • ILLUSTRATED BY CHRIS AGUIRRE

Random House New York

ISBN 978-0-593-57024-1 (trade) — ISBN 978-0-593-57025-8 (ebook)

Printed in the United States of America

10 9 8 7 6 5 4 3 2 1

Random House Children's Books supports the First Amendment and celebrates the right to read.

THE CHUMASH TRIBE

Spirit Rangers is inspired by the Santa Ynez Band of Chumash Indians, a federally recognized Native American tribe. Xus National Park is based in part on the creeks, forests, wildflowers, and mountains of the tribe's ancestral lands. *Xus* means "bear" in the Samala Chumash language. Many of the characters in this series are inspired by the stories of Samala Chumash matriarch Maria Solares.

The Santa Ynez Band of Chumash Indians is a self-governing sovereign nation and maintains economic self-sufficiency through business development, investments, and the Chumash Casino Resort. The word *Chumash* means "bead money people," and the tribe was known for its sophisticated trading system, made possible by plank canoes, or tomol. A maritime people, the Chumash thrived as boat makers, basket weavers, rock artists, fishermen, and astronomers.

Today the Chumash offer a variety of cultural enrichment programs that maintain and advance the culture and Samala language. Chumash pride and identity is visible through classes and annual events, such as the Chumash Inter-Tribal Pow-Wow, Chumash Culture Day, and Camp Kalawashaq for Chumash youth. Through these ongoing programs and cultural sharing, the Chumash are dedicated to preserving the lands, language, culture, and people.

SAMALA GLOSSARY AND PRONUNCIATION GUIDE

cho-ho (good) — cho-ho

haku (hello) — ha-koo

tuhuy (rain) — tuh-hoo-ee

xus (bear) — hoos

THE COWLITZ TRIBE

The Cowlitz Indian Tribe is a federally recognized Native American tribe located in the Pacific Northwest. Following its recognition in 2000, the tribe focused on business development and has a major casino-resort on its reservation in Ridgefield, Washington, which is of major economic benefit to surrounding counties. Documents from the 1800s describe Cowlitz territory as a placement of four stronghold areas representing cultures suited to mountains, prairies, and lowland rivers. The Cowlitz people were cedar and salmon people, harvesting many species of fish from river systems, as well as wild prairie vegetables and berries from higher elevations. Cowlitz women were famous for their skill in cedar weaving, especially basketry. Cowlitz men were master carvers of cedar and other evergreen and deciduous trees. Their design of the shovel-nosed canoe made them adept at controlling the rivers in a sophisticated trade enterprise. Because their lands contained more prairie than most Salish tribes, the Cowlitz were excellent horse breeders and trainers. The people were multilingual, with the predominant languages being Cowlitz Coast Salish and Sahaptin. Diseases brought by non-native people reduced the population beginning in the 1830s. Today, there are approximately 4,500 enrolled members of the Cowlitz Tribe. The modern Cowlitz Tribe is culturally strong and continues to build its business portfolio. It is also concentrating on bringing the Cowlitz Coast Salish language back after a long dormancy.

Welcome to Xus National Park located in Chumash territory! This is where the Skycedar family lives. The family is Indigenous to Chumash and Cowlitz lands. The Chumash Tribe is in Southern California and the Cowlitz Tribe is in Washington.

Kodi, Summer, and Eddy Skycedar love their culture, the park, and the spirits who secretly live here with them.

Mom and Dad have a special surprise for the kids. As of today,
Kodi, Summer, and Eddy are Junior Park Rangers!
"Cho-ho! This is the best day of my life!" cheers Kodi.
"Eee! I'm so happy!" Summer squeals as she dances.

Eddy hides in his hoodie pajamas. "Are you sure we're ready?" he worries.
"You're more ready than you think," promises Mom.
But Eddy doesn't think he can be a park ranger. Even though he gets dressed
to go out, he hides his badge in his pocket.

It's time to open the park! The Skycedar family hikes to the Ranger Station.

The sun is shining, and the spirits have come out to play. Nothing can ruin the kids' first day as Junior Park Rangers!

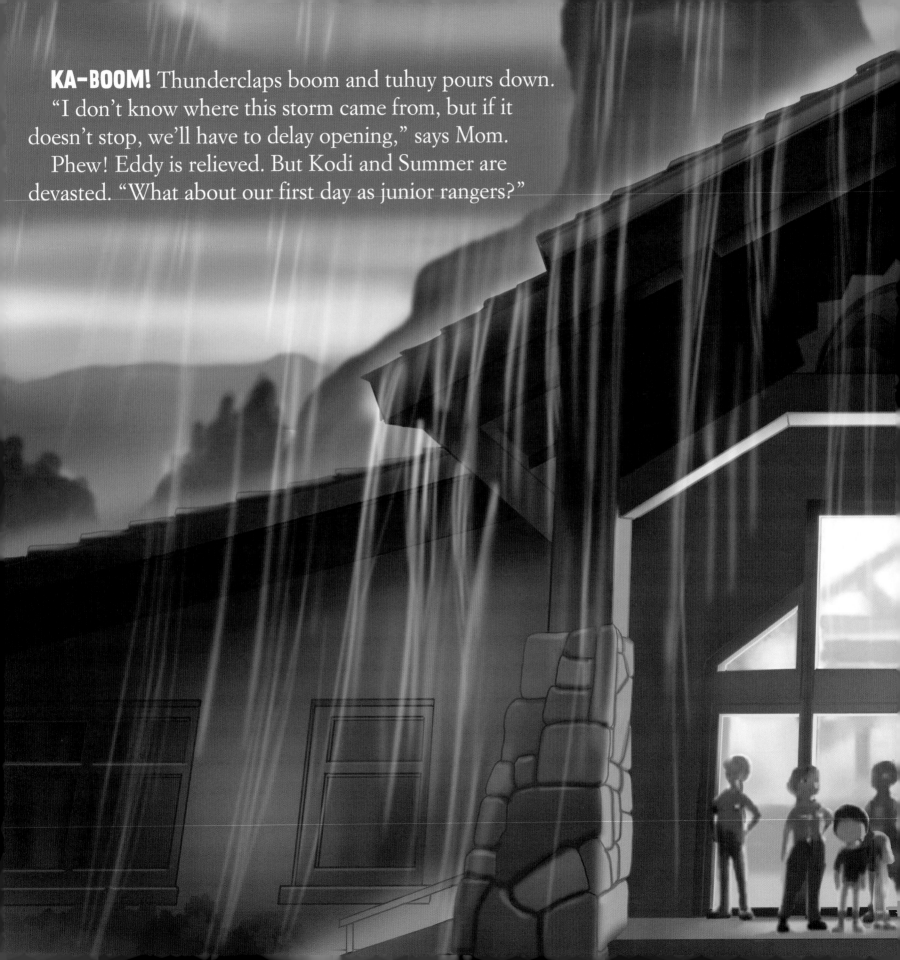

KA-BOOM! Thunderclaps boom and tuhuy pours down. "I don't know where this storm came from, but if it doesn't stop, we'll have to delay opening," says Mom. Phew! Eddy is relieved. But Kodi and Summer are devasted. "What about our first day as junior rangers?"

"Maybe the spirits know where the storm came from," Kodi suggests.
"Only one way to find out," Summer answers with a smile.
Eddy gulps. "Okay. *Maybe* the spirits can help stop this scary storm."
The kids sprint to their tree house, where they

. . . transform!
Kodi turns into a bear.
Summer turns into a red-tailed hawk.
And Eddy turns into a turtle.

They're Spirit Ranger ready!
The siblings are now in
Spirit Park. They can see the
spirits who live here.

In Spirit Park, the storm is even stronger.

"C-c-can we go home?" asks Eddy, hiding in his shell.

"We're rangers now, remember?" says Kodi. "It's up to us to protect the park."

Summer notices that the clouds are moving *really* fast. She realizes that those aren't clouds at all. They must be . . .

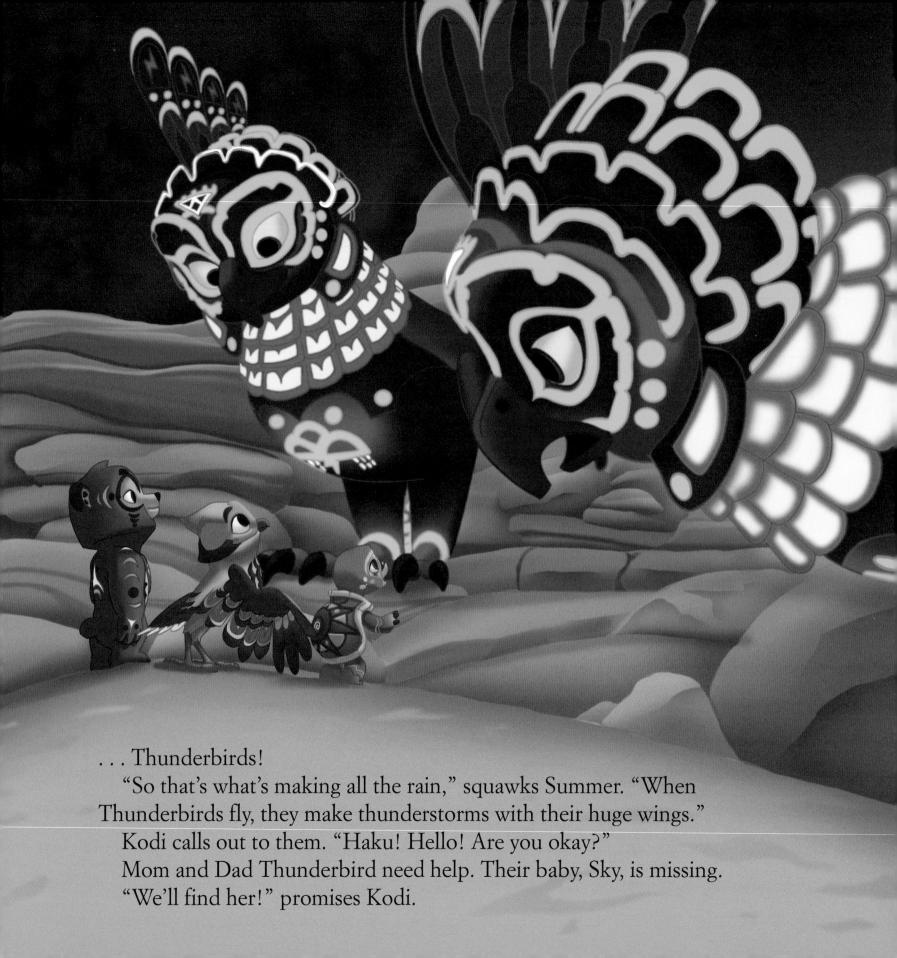

. . . Thunderbirds!

"So that's what's making all the rain," squawks Summer. "When Thunderbirds fly, they make thunderstorms with their huge wings."

Kodi calls out to them. "Haku! Hello! Are you okay?"

Mom and Dad Thunderbird need help. Their baby, Sky, is missing.

"We'll find her!" promises Kodi.

The kids search every crook and cranny of Spirit Park,
but there's no sign of Sky anywhere. Where could she be?

BOOM! More thunder rumbles through the park.
Eddy withdraws into his shell. "I'm too scared," he admits.
"I'm not ready to be a ranger. . . ."

Summer and Kodi huddle around Eddy. "What's wrong?" they ask.

"Mom and Dad make being a ranger look so easy, but it's a big job. What if I mess up?" he asks.

"Learning is part of the job," says Summer.

"We can face any storm if we're together," adds Kodi.

Suddenly lightning snaps across the sky. Kodi wraps Summer in a bear hug. The storm is scary!

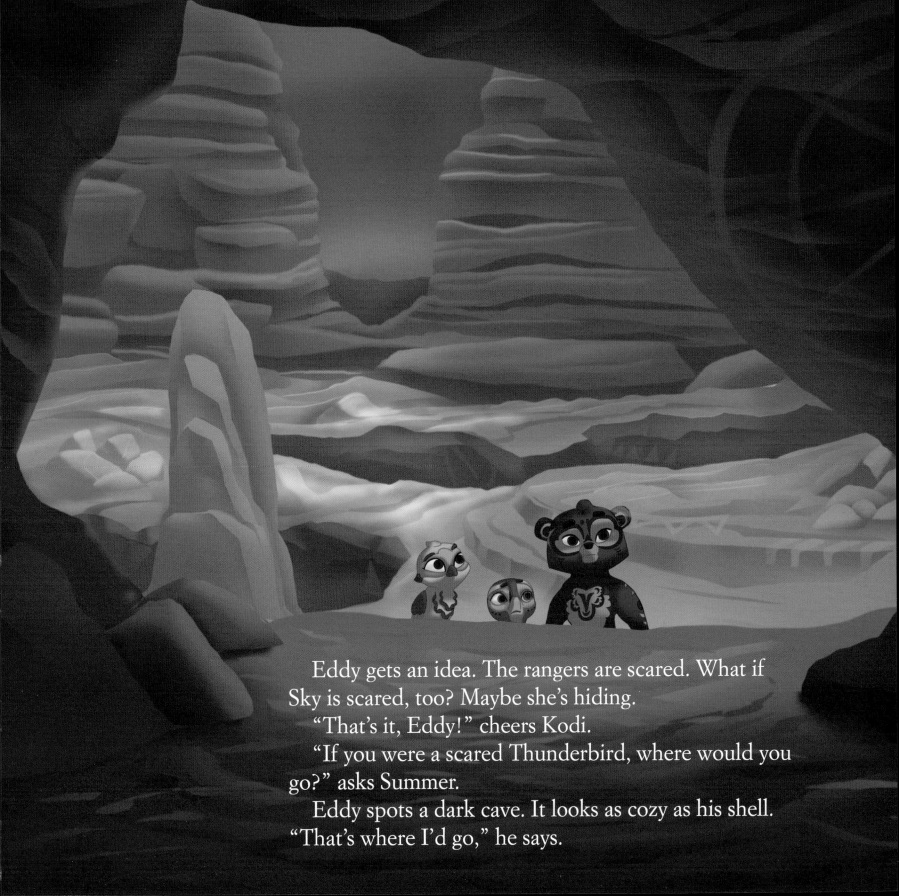

Eddy gets an idea. The rangers are scared. What if Sky is scared, too? Maybe she's hiding.

"That's it, Eddy!" cheers Kodi.

"If you were a scared Thunderbird, where would you go?" asks Summer.

Eddy spots a dark cave. It looks as cozy as his shell. "That's where I'd go," he says.

The kids climb to the cave and find a bright feather.
Sky must be inside!
With Summer and Kodi's support, Eddy bravely
enters the cave.

Eddy spots a fuzzy baby Thunderbird. She nervously pokes her head out of her hiding place. It's Sky!

"Boom boom . . . scary," she says, trying to hide from the thunder.

Eddy tells her he knows *exactly* how she feels. "Learning is part of the job," says Eddy. "The storm is just your parents flapping their wings."

"Flap flap?" asks Sky.

"That's right! See? You're more ready than you think you are." Eddy holds out his hand for her.

Sky takes his hand, and they step out of the cave.
"You did it, Eddy! She's out of the cave," cheers Summer.
"And you came out of your shell," says Kodi, smiling.
"Mama? Dada?" asks Sky as she searches the clouds.

The rangers call to the Thunderbirds: **caw-caw**!

The Thunderbirds fly over. Sky rushes to snuggle her parents.
"Thank you, Spirit Rangers," squawks Dad Thunderbird.
"She was a little scared," says Eddy. "But now she's ready to face any storm."

Kodi, Summer, and Eddy wave goodbye as the Thunderbirds fly home. The clouds part and the sun shines bright. The storm is gone!

Back in Xus Park, Dad wonders how the storm disappeared so suddenly. It's a mystery. "It's almost like magic," Mom says.

Soon the kids join them in their junior ranger uniforms. "Does this mean we can open the park?" asks Summer.

"We're ready if you three are. What do you say?" asks Mom.

"Eddy is ready!" says Eddy. He proudly pins his badge to his sleeve.
Eddy knows that he and his siblings will be amazing Junior Park Rangers!